CONTENTS

MINIBEASTS!

Just Like Bugs

Busy like a butterfly
buzzy like a bee
shiny like a firefly
itchy like a flea

Spotty like a ladybird
stripy like a wasp
zippy like a dragonfly
flappy like a moth

Scratchy like a beetle
tiny like an ant
how many bugs here?
Hey, let's count!

One for the butterfly
two for the bee
three for the firefly
four for the flea

Five for the ladybird
six for the wasp
seven for the dragonfly
eight for the moth

Nine for the beetle
ten for the ant –
double high five
it's a ten bug count!

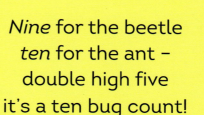

4

It's a Bug!

If it jiggles just a little
or its home is in the mud
or it wiggles down its middle...

oh, indeed – it's a bug!

If it scuttles or it rustles
or it leaps upon a rug
or it bustles in a meadow...

yes, siree – it's a bug!

If it scratches or it scrabbles
or its meal is made of muck
or it shuffles in the shadows...

OMG – it's a
BUG!

We call them 'bugs'. Scientists call them **INSECTS**. They're found all over the world – in forests, deserts, gardens, farms, homes, everywhere. How many do you think there are altogether? Aim high! Only some 10 QUINTILLION – that's many, many millions of billions of bugs!

Hey, Little Bug!

gimme a hug!

gimme a hug!

gimme a hug!

gimme a hug!

gimme a hug!

gimme a hug!

Hey little bug - how do you hug - or cuddle or kiss your mum or sis - with all those arms and legs and things - and wiggly bits and wobbly wings? For however hairy or creepy or scary even the ugliest bug needs a H U G !

So what are **BUGS** (or INSECTS) exactly? They're little creatures with 2 pairs of wings, 3 pairs of legs and 3 main body parts – a head, thorax and abdomen, plus 1 pair of twitchy antennae on their heads to help them feel and smell their way around.

antennae

head

thorax

abdomen

fANTastic!

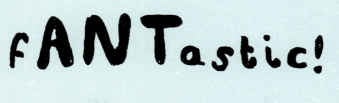

There's nothing wrong
with being small

so titchy that
the grass seems tall

more weeny than
a leaf or twig

so tiny that
a bee seems big.

That's how it is
and we don't mind.

We're stronger than
you humankind

and just as smart
we think you'll find.

How can we lift
a giANT stick?

That's because we're
fANTastic!

ANTS have the biggest of all bug brains. And though a single ant may not be too clever, together a colony of ants can do incredible things, even though they don't have ears and many don't have eyes. Like wasps and bees, ants are very social creatures and live and work together to thrive.

7

Grasshopper

Grasshopper
  fast hopper

zipping nipping
  past hopper

high hopper
  grasshopper

      long
   day
all

Here it comes
  again hopper

bouncing all
  the way hopper

non-stopper
  grasshopper

     G O N E !
   going
going

BOING!

Hoppy frogs are bouncing high
as happy hares go bounding by
but here are bugs that touch the sky

BOING! BOING! BOING!

The human eye can barely see
they're smaller than a tiny pea
they soar about so secretly

BOING! BOING! BOING!

They're itchy, titchy, flicky fleas
they leap about, and with such ease
they're on the move from beast to beast –

BOING! BOING! BOING!

From yappy dogs to sassy cats
they dine just fine on YOU in fact –
for yikes, they like a human snack!

BOING! BOING! BOING!

So when you spot a flea (or few)
this is what you'll need to do
hop it – like a KANGAROO!

BOING! BOING! BOING!

Bugs get around in all kinds of ways. Flying, leaping, crawling, walking, even up walls and trees. Some bugs can go sdrawkcab as easily as forwards! Both **FLEAS** and **GRASSHOPPERS** leap so high as they have extra-long back legs. Some insects – like diving beetles and water boatmen – are able to swim, while pond skaters can actually walk on the surface of water. Skills!

9

Butterfly

What better
than a butterfly
to brighten up
a summer sky?

And what a thrill
when it lands
soft as breath
upon your hand.

Hey there,
little flappy guy –
thanks a lot
for popping by!

10

Leafy Lunch

Nibble, nibble
wriggle, wriggle

gobble, gobble
wiggle, wiggle

non-stop
munch, munch

caterpillar's
having lunch!

Yum, yum
hooray

lunch lasts
all day!

A **CATERPILLAR** is one greedy grub! Also known as a larva, it first eats the egg it hatched out of, then the leaf it's standing on, and from there any other leaf it can wiggle over to!

The lives of both the **BUTTERFLY** and the moth are in four parts (known as a life cycle) – first there's the egg, next the caterpillar, then the pupa and finally the adult butterfly.
How many legs do caterpillars have? As with all insects, it has just three front pairs, as all the others are for decoration only!

The Moth and the Moon

Who wants to go to the moon...? she sang,
Who wants to go to the moon...?
Its light's so bright, so cool, so blue.
I'm hypnotised all night. Aren't you?
I want to go to the moon, she sang –
I want to go to the moon!

The bugs all came
from high and low.
In turn, they told
her not to go.

It's far too far too far! sang one.
Your wings might burn – too near the sun!
Together they warned, *you haven't the puff!*
It's cold. You'll freeze. Come back, dear Moth!

Yet up she went,
but flippered about
and failed to even
reach a cloud.

Then stopped. Mid air –
let out a sigh....
and down she drifted
through the sky.

Since then each night
she's found a light
that causes her
such great delight.

A lamp maybe.
A flickery flame.
She'll dance away
till break of day.

For Moth you see has changed her tune –
With lights on earth who needs the moon?
They're bright as sun and just as fun!
Who wants to go to the moon...? she sang,
Who wants to go to the moon...?

Ever seen a **MOTH** flippity-flapping around a lamp at night? Scientists believe moths do this as they mistake these lights for the moon and the stars that they navigate by.

Want an eye-watering moth fact? In Thailand there's a moth that drinks the tears of elephants. What's it called? The Elephant Tear Moth of course!

What Can It Be...?

That
stripy-jumper,
flower-lover, happy-
zzz   hummer, must-be-Summer,   zzz
zzzzzz   *garden-grower, come-and-goer,*   zzzzzz
zzzzzzzz   *garden-grower, come-and-goer,*   zzzzzzzzz
zzzzzz   black-and-yella, busy-fella,   zzzzzz
zzzzzzz   *planet-aider, pollinator,*   zzzzzzz
zz   super-stinger, syrup-bringer?   zz
When it's sunny, pop
and see - can you
spot a HONEY
BEE
?

Everyone knows that
BEES make honey...but do they?
Actually, only honeybees do.
All the other 20,000 types –
from bumblebees to carpenter
bees and dwarf bees – don't.

FAB FACT TIME
It's only female
wasps and bees
that can sting.

14

What On Earth's a...

One **W**oefully

under-**A**ppreciated

pe**S**t-controlling,

Pollinating bug!

?

We know that bees do a great deal of good for the world – but hang on – so do **WASPS**! Bees, wasps and a whole bunch of other flying bugs are all active pollinators, helping to produce everything from fruit and vegetables to nuts, tea and cocoa beans.

Bye Bye, Ladybird

I'm spotty
I'm dotty
I'm lovely
and red

I live
in your garden
a leaf
is my bed

I'm tiny
I'm titchy
I've come to say
"Hi!"

But I'm
in a hurry
so I'll say
"Bye bye!"

Like bumblebees and some butterflies, **LADYBIRDS** hibernate in the winter months, so you may find them huddled together in the corner of a window frame where it's snug and warm.

Dear Firefly...

do tell me why

you shine at night?
Do you store light,

a scoop of sun
inside your tum?

How cool are you?
Wish I could too!

FIREFLIES can 'talk', but they flash their lights to do so! Ants 'talk' by smell, treehoppers by vibrating their bodies and honeybees by dancing. Creative!

Ladybirds and FIREFLIES are actually types of beetle, not birds or flies! Weird, eh?

A Day in the Life of a Dung Beetle

There is only one beetle
up with the sun beetle
stuff to be done beetle

DUNG! DUNG! DUNG!

Waiting for the drop beetle
get it while it's hot beetle
oh, what a lot beetle

DUNG! DUNG! DUNG!

Let the work begin beetle
give it everything beetle
gotta make it spin beetle

DUNG! DUNG! DUNG!

Time to head away beetle
backwards all the way beetle
rolling through the day beetle

DUNG! DUNG! DUNG!

Now it's getting dark beetle
following the stars beetle
clever-and-a-half beetle

DUNG! DUNG! DUNG!

Strongest bug there is beetle
best recycle whizz beetle
in the eco-biz beetle

DUNG! DUNG! DUNG!

The world's strongest insects? **DUNG BEETLES**!
Those dung balls that they craft and then roll
backwards are over 1,000 times their body weight.
So why dung? When large herbivorous mammals drop those
plops there are tiny amounts of plants, grasses, leaves
and fruit inside the dung that the beetle will eat. These
beetles also use the dung to lay their eggs in.

Fancy a rotten joke? What's brown and sounds
like a bell? DUNG!

Me No Dragon...

me no fly
but you could
call me

summer-sprite

silky-wing

super-nippy

zippy-thing

soul-a-flicker

heart-a-flutter

shiny-shimmer

like-no-other

even little-whizz-on-by

or maybe

stick with

DRAGONFLY?

You've probably seen a **DRAGONFLY** darting here and there next to a pond, lake or river. But did you know that their young can spend up to two years underwater?

20

The Spider and the Fly

Said the spider to the fly,
"You're a funny little guy,

yet I find I love you so."
"So set me free," said Fly. "Oh no!"

said Spider, "here is fine.
Let's relax and soon we'll dine."

"Dine?" said Fly. "There's no food here!"
Spider grinned. "It's *you*, my dear…"

Ready to be confused? Dragonflies are NOT true flies! Nor are mayflies, fireflies or butterflies. To be a true **FLY**, an insect has to use one pair of wings to fly with, and another to use for balance – like house flies, bluebottles, fruit flies, even mosquitos. Like 'em or not, flies are incredible. Look at their googly 'compound' eyes – they're made of thousands of mini-eyes! What's more, they rid the world of all kinds of disgusting stuff like poo and rotting matter. *Phew!*

Bed Bugs

Night-night, sleep tight. Don't let the bed bugs bite.

We love to bite
oh yes, it's true
if you were a bug
then so might you

When you're at play
we're starved all day
when you drop off
we have our scoff

So life is good
and that's for sure
but hey, you humans –

*PLEASE
DON'T
SNORE!*

22

Mosquito, Mosquito...

of all minibeast-o
I like you the least-o

Just look at my feet-o
you've had quite a feast-o

It's time to finito,
MOSQUITO!

THE most unpopular bug? HAS to be the fly that we call the **MOSQUITO**! Ready for a yuck-fest? When those mozzies bite us humans they leave their saliva in our skin – so our bodies fight against it, and by doing so it creates bumps that itch. Other beastly bugs? Ticks, headlice, cockroaches – and our nasty night-time blood-sucker chums, **BED BUGS**. Ooof!

As beastly as they can be, we need bugs. And we can help them by buying or building BUG HOTELS. These are safe places for bugs to hibernate, escape from danger, lay their eggs and raise their young.

23

The Mini and the Many Beasts!

Many are
the minibeasts
there's plenty
of these diddy beasts

They're little critters
pesky pests
invertebrates –
like insects

Earwigs
and bed bugs
centipedes
and sea slugs

Spiders
and dragonflies
jellyfish
and woodlice

Sea, tree,
air, ground
minibeasts
are all around

Did you know
there's more of these
than every other
type of beast?

If you don't
believe a word –
check 'em out
around the world!

How Many Minibeasts?

A *stampede* of millipedes?
A *festival* of fleas?
An *earful* of earwigs?
A *business* of bees?

A *rock 'n roll* of dung beetles?
A *squadron* of wasps?
A *scuttling* of ladybirds?
A *discotheque* of moths?

A *fidgeting* of earth worms?
A *nastiness* of nits?
A *beastliness* of minibeasts?
This poem makes me *ITCH*!

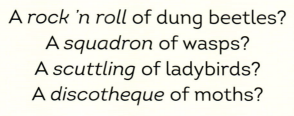

MINIBEASTS is the name given to all those little creatures that include insects as well as slugs, snails, worms, millipedes, spiders and even jellyfish and starfish! All minibeasts – bugs included – are invertebrates, which means they don't have backbones – but actually, most of the world's creatures are invertebrates!

A Sticky Riddle

Wherever
I
roam
I'm
close
to
home
and
leave
a
silver
trail –
in
mist
or
frost
I'm
never
lost
because
I
am
a
. . .
?

Wriggly-wigglies like **SNAILS**, as well as slugs and worms, are not bugs, but they are in the huge MINIBEAST family. Plus they're nothing like insects, apart from being small. Did you know that slugs used to have shells once upon a time? Or that snails often have two hearts? Ahhh...

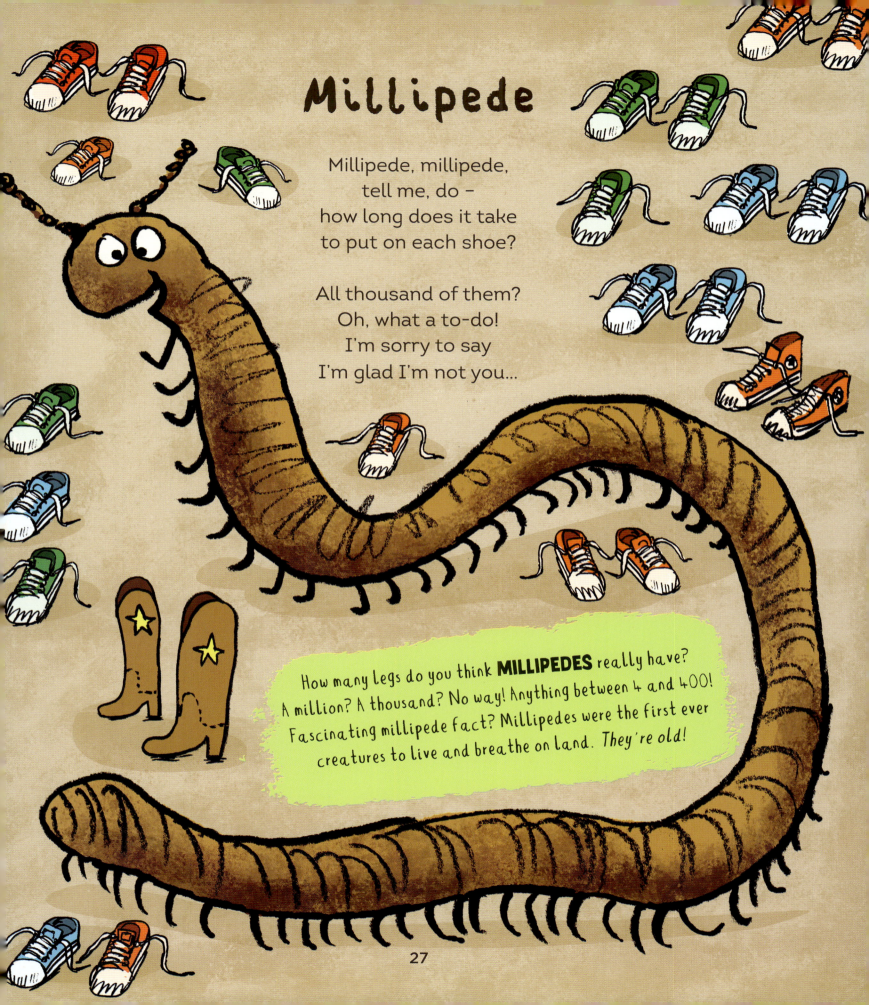

Millipede

Millipede, millipede,
tell me, do –
how long does it take
to put on each shoe?

All thousand of them?
Oh, what a to-do!
I'm sorry to say
I'm glad I'm not you...

How many legs do you think **MILLIPEDES** really have? A million? A thousand? No way! Anything between 4 and 400! Fascinating millipede fact? Millipedes were the first ever creatures to live and breathe on land. They're old!

Have You Seen a...

Scuttling or **S**currying away?

Wrapping sticky silk around its **P**rey?

Dangling down a th**I**n, stringy thread?

Shuffling in the sha**D**ows of a shed?

Assembling a w**E**b for a bed?

Or just for a laugh – lu**R**king in your bath...

?

Let's talk numbers. **SPIDERS** not only have 8 legs, they also have 8 eyes. But they can build a great many more webs in a lifetime – up to 200!

SOAP

YUCKY SPIDER FACT? Female spiders often eat their mates. Woah!

'Pig' In Space!

The toughest critter
of them all?

It's micro-tiny,
weeny-small.

Has stubby legs.
A piggy face.

Can live in oceans,
ice or space...

the tardigrade –
it's truly ace!

And without water,
food or air

it will thrive
most anywhere.

Soon it might just
leave the Earth

to travel round
the universe.

It's evolution's
champ to date...

we salute you,
tardigrade!

TARDIGRADES
are maybe THE most amazing
of all living creatures. Though
almost invisible to the eye, they
can survive in extreme heat and
cold – even in space – and
without food for weeks.
Respect!

For Neal Layton – for bringing all his utterly
bugly brilliance to our book.
And dung heaps of gratitude to Darren Mann
at the Oxford University Museum of Natural History
for all his minibeastly expertise.
JC

For wordsmith James Carter
and young story maker Maja
NL

Text copyright © James Carter 2025
Illustrations copyright © Neal Layton 2025
First published in Great Britain and the USA in 2025 by
Otter-Barry Books, Little Orchard, Burley Gate, Herefordshire, HR1 3QS
www.otterbarrybooks.com

A catalogue record for this book is available from the British Library
Designed by Arianna Osti

ISBN 978-1-915659-50-7
Illustrated with pencil, ink and digital media

Set in Gotham
Printed in China

9 8 7 6 5 4 3 2 1

FSC
www.fsc.org

MIX
Paper | Supporting
responsible forestry
FSC® C104723